Diplodocus
Dih-PLOD-o-kus

Camarasaurus
KAM-ah-rah-sawr-us

Apatosaurus
Ah-PAT-o-sawr-us

Ceratosaurus
Sayr-AT-o-sawr-us

Stegosaurus
STEG-o-sawr-us

Allosaurus
AL-o-sawr-us

Camptosaurus
KAMP-to-sawr-us

Library of Congress Cataloging in Publication Data
Threadgall, Colin.
Dinosaur fright/by Colin Threadgall.—1st U.S. ed.
p.   cm.
Summary: When bullying brachiosaurs invade the territory of
smaller dinosaurs, a little nanosaur devises a clever plan.
ISBN 0-688-11733-3 (TR).—ISBN 0-688-11734-1 (LE)
[1. Dinosaurs—Fiction.]   I. Title.
PZ7.T4115Di   1993   [E]—dc20   91-40049   CIP   AC

1   3   5   7   9   10   8   6   4   2

First U.S. edition, 1993

Colin Threadgall

DINOSAUR FRIGHT

TAMBOURINE BOOKS

New York

A long time ago, dinosaurs lived together in a forest by a lake.

One day there was a noise like thunder and the ground trembled...THUMP! THUMP! THUMP!

It was a herd of giant Brachiosaurus.

"Go away!" cried the other dinosaurs.

But the Brachiosaurus only laughed as they crashed and bashed about.

They jumped into the lake, and flooded everything with their enormous splashes.

They reared and stamped and bellowed.

"You go away," they boomed. "We like it here."

Little Nanosaurus crept up behind them. "Beware," he said, "you might upset the monster."

"MONSTER!" roared the Brachiosaurus all together. "We're bigger than any monster."

The other dinosaurs were puzzled.
"But there isn't any monster," they said.
"There will be tonight," said Nanosaurus.

He told them what to do. First they collected spiders'
webs and stuck them on to the leafy tops of three fallen trees.

Then, when darkness fell, they caught as many fireflies as they could,

and stuck them on to the spiders' webs.

When it was truly dark they took the trees to the top of a hill.

Below them the Brachiosaurus lay sleeping.

The three trees were placed in position.

Then the dinosaurs howled and shrieked and roared and stamped and shook the trees. They made a dreadful noise.

The Brachiosaurus woke in fright. They saw a great fiery mouth and two enormous glowing eyes above them.

There was a monster! A huge monster!

Up they jumped and away they galumphed, as fast as they possibly could.

And they never, never came back.